Catherine and Laurence Anholt's

BIG BOOK of Little Children

For Daniel Damodar

First published individually as *What I Like* (1991), *Kids* (1992), *Here Come the Babies* (1993),
What Makes Me Happy? (1994) and *Catherine and Laurence Anholt's Big Book of Families* (1998)
by Walker Books Ltd, 87 Vauxhall Walk, London SE11 5HJ

This edition published 2005

2 4 6 8 10 9 7 5 3 1

This book has been typeset in Bembo

Printed in China

British Library Cataloguing in Publication Data:
a catalogue record for this book is available from the British Library

ISBN 1-84428-516-2

www.walkerbooks.co.uk

Catherine and Laurence Anholt's

BiG BooK of Little Children

WALKER BOOKS
AND SUBSIDIARIES
LONDON • BOSTON • SYDNEY • AUCKLAND

Contents

Very Little Children

Here come the babies!

Babies in boxes, babies in boots, babies on backs

Babies in socks, babies in suits, babies in sacks

Babies everywhere!

Babies in coats, babies in cribs, babies with cats

Babies in boats, babies in bibs, babies with bats

What are babies like?

Babies kick and babies crawl,

Slide their potties down the hall.

Babies smile and babies yell,

This one has a funny smell.

What do babies play with?

Bobbles and bows, fingers and toes,

Shoes and hats, sleeping cats,

Frizzy hair,

saggy bear,

Empty box,

Daddy's socks.

What's in a pram?

nappy bag

favourite rag

food to cook

picture book

floppy bunny

something funny

one shoe

baby too

What does a baby do?

hug

hold

hide

sleep

smile

slide

jumble   juggle   jump

bang   burp   bump

totter   tumble   throw

gurgle   giggle   grow

What do lots of babies do?

One baby bouncing on her brother's knee,

Two in a play-pen, three by the sea,

Four babies yelling while their
mummies try to talk,

Five babies, holding hands,
learning how to walk.

Little Children's Likes and Loves

What I like is…

ice-cream

a funny dream

my thermos flask

my monster mask

I love...

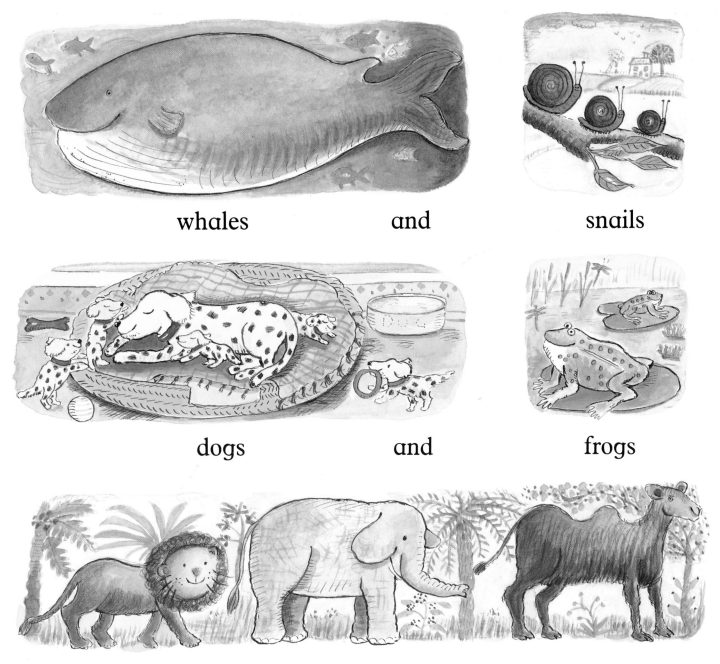

whales   and   snails

dogs   and   frogs

lots of animals

I don't like…

getting lost

What I like is...

time to play

a holiday

toys

(some) boys

waking early

hair all curly

I don't like…

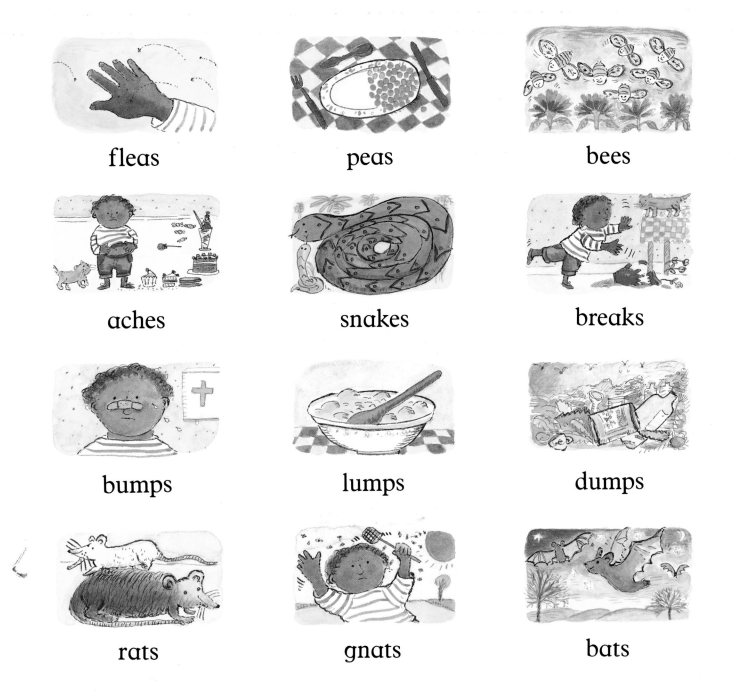

fleas

peas

bees

aches

snakes

breaks

bumps

lumps

dumps

rats

gnats

bats

I love…

playing the fool   a swimming pool   nursery school

How Little Children Feel

What makes me laugh?

tickly toes

a big red nose

being rude

silly food

acting crazy

my friend Maisie

What makes me cry?

wasps that sting

a fall from a swing

wobbly wheels

head over heels

What makes me pleased?

Look how much I've grown!

I can do it on my own!

What makes me sad?

Rain, rain, every day.

No one wants to let me play.

Someone special's far away.

What makes us excited?

A roller-coaster ride

Here comes the bride!

The monster's on his way!

A party day

What makes me cross?

Days when buttons won't go straight
and I want to stay up late
and I hate what's on my plate…
Why won't anybody wait?

What makes us all happy?

singing a song

skipping along

windy weather

finding a feather and...

Being together.

What Little Children Do

We are the kids!

Big kids, small kids, tiny kids, tall kids

Happy kids, grumpy kids, skinny kids, dumpy kids

Look out, here we come!

Slow kids, quick kids, healthy kids, sick kids

Smooth kids, hairy kids, cute kids, scary kids

What are kids like?

Kids are silly, kids are funny,

Kids have noses that are runny.

Some kids wash but some are smelly,

Both kinds like to watch the telly.

What do kids do?

mix

mess

muddle

comfort

kiss

cuddle

laugh

leap

lick

poke

push

pick

scratch

scream

scrawl

break

bellow

bawl

Where do kids hide?

Seven in a bed, six in a box,

Five behind curtains, four behind clocks,

Three up a tree, two down a hole.

Here is a kid who hid in some coal.

What do kids make?

Houses with blankets,

Mountains on stairs,

Seas out of carpets,

Trains out of chairs.

What are kids' secrets?

A ladybird in a matchbox,

A letter under a bed,

A horrid pie in a horrible place,

A den behind a shed.

What are nasty kids like?

They pull your hair, they call you names,
They tell you lies, they spoil your games,
They draw on walls, scream on the floor.
Nasty kids want more, more, more.

What are nice kids like?

They make you laugh, they hold your hand,
Nice kids always understand.
They share their toys, they let you play,
They chase the nasty kids away.

What do kids dream of?

A ladder to the moon,

A candy tree in bloom,

Riding a flying fish,

Having anything they wish.

Little Children's Families

Families together

Families laughing,

families sharing,

families loving,

families shoving.

Families teasing,

families tugging,

families helping,

families hugging.

Mums and Dads

Mummy, mummy, sweet as honey,
Busy as a bee,
Buzzing off to earn some money,
Buzzing home to me.

Dads have ...
Big hands and baseball caps,
Ties and tattoos,
Shoulders to ride on,
Shoes like canoes.
Some dads build houses
But can't make the bed;
This dad is hairy
Except on his head.

My mum says:
　　Brush your hair,
　　Sit still, say "please",
　　Wash your hands,

　　　　Your ears, your knees,
　　　　　You've left your clothes
　　　　All in a heap,
　　　　　Don't pick your nose,

Now go to sleep!

Brothers and Sisters

This afternoon I told my mother,
"I've changed my mind about my brother,
I'd rather have that model plane,
Will you send him back again?"

I'm the middle sister,
I think it's really mean,
I'm squashed in-between
Like a tinned sardine.
I'm the filling in the sandwich,
That's what I am –
Mum says I'm sweet
So perhaps I'm the jam.

Sisters squeak and sisters shriek,
Slam the door, refuse to speak.
Sisters sneak and sisters peek,
 Then turn all soft
  and kiss your cheek.

Grannies and Grandads

My granny has …

Two old dogs

A pile of logs

Shelves of books

Some fishing hooks

Aching feet

A special treat

Jars and tins

Needles and pins

A walking stick

Clocks that tick

A favourite chair

Time to spare

In the woods with Grandad,
Through the winter snow –
One of us is fast,
One of us is slow.

In the woods with Grandad,
Walking on our own –
Grandad keeps on smiling:
"My, how much you've grown!"

In the woods with Grandad,
The sun goes down like gold –
One of us is young,
One of us is old.

Busy Families

Skirts and shirts and dressing gowns—
The wind begins to blow—
They're like a family upside-down
Dancing in a row!

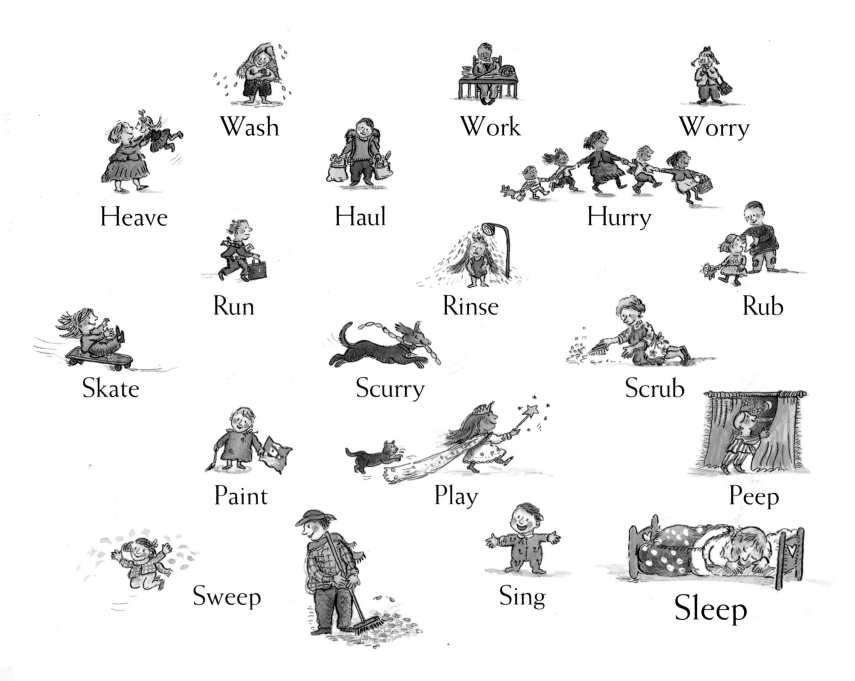

Wash

Work

Worry

Heave

Haul

Hurry

Run

Rinse

Rub

Skate

Scurry

Scrub

Paint

Play

Peep

Sweep

Sing

Sleep

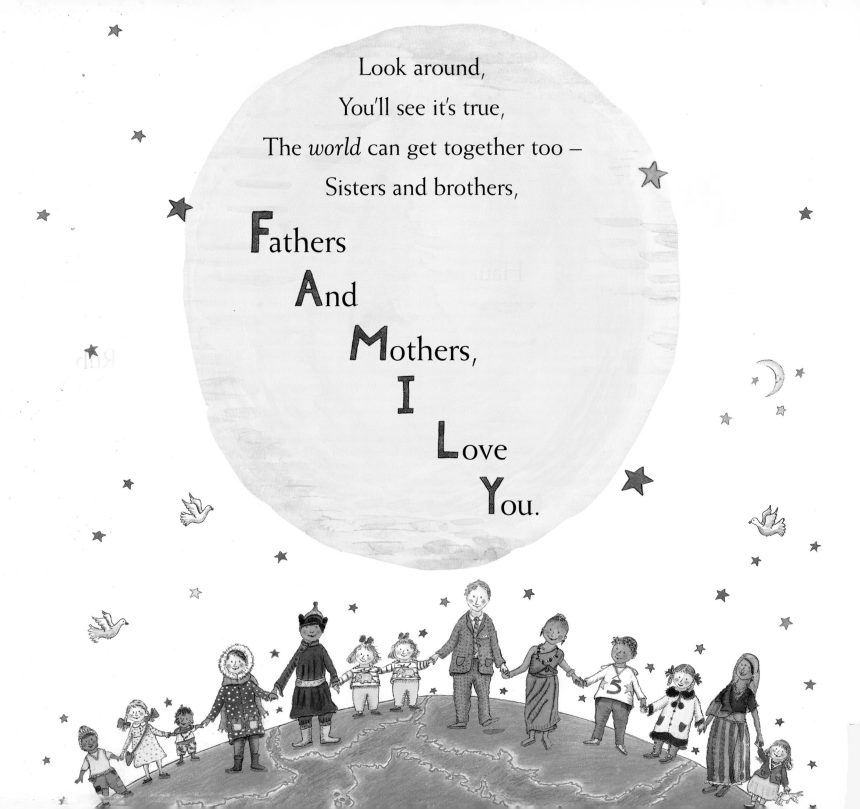

Look around,
You'll see it's true,
The *world* can get together too –
Sisters and brothers,

Fathers

And

Mothers,

I

Love

You.